GOOD FOOD, GOOD FOR EARTH

BY DARLENE R. STILLE

The Child's World

Published by The Child's World®
1980 Lookout Drive • Mankato, MN 56003-1705
800-599-READ • www.childsworld.com

PHOTO CREDITS
Yenwen Lu/iStockphoto, cover, 1; Fotolia, 5, 7, 29; Monkey Business
Images/Shutterstock Images, 9; Glenda M. Powers/Shutterstock
Images, 11; Shutterstock Images, 13; iStockphoto, 15, 19; Bigstock, 17;
Eric Michaud/iStockphoto, 21; Jakub Jirsák/iStockphoto, 23; Ilya D.
Gridnev/Shutterstock Images, 25; Nayashkova Olga/Shutterstock
Images, 27

CONTENT CONSULTANT
Karen O'Connor, co-owner, Mother Earth Gardens,
Minneapolis, Minnesota

ACKNOWLEDGMENTS
The Child's World®: Mary Berendes, Publishing Director
The Design Lab: Design
Red Line Editorial: Editorial direction

ISBN: 978-1-60973-173-1
LCCN: 2011927672

Printed in the United States of America in Mankato, MN
July, 2011
PA02090

TABLE OF CONTENTS

FRESHER FOOD, BETTER FOOD

Where does the food you eat come from? If you answered "a store," you would not be wrong. But there is a lot more to the story.

Big corporations grow and raise much of our food. On these corporate farms, wheat, corn, and other crops grow with the help of chemical fertilizers and pesticides. Often, chickens, pigs, and cattle are crowded together in small areas. These kinds of farms are called **factory farms**.

Many people do not like factory farms. Environmentalists are concerned that the tons of chemicals used on these farms wash into water supplies. Some fear that the antibiotics fed to the animals could be harmful to people.

Animals are often crowded together in small spaces on factory farms.

These people think there are better ways to grow and buy food. Buying **organic** food, or food grown without chemicals, is one way. Another way is to eat food grown by local farmers. Buying locally grown food saves energy that would be used to store, refrigerate, and ship processed foods.

VISIT A FARMERS' MARKET

Ask a grown-up to take you to a **farmers' market** that sells locally grown food. You will see tables, bushel baskets, and boxes set up and filled with fruits and vegetables. You can buy fruits and vegetables that may have been picked early that morning. Now that's fresh!

WHY?

Most of the foods sold at a farmers' market are grown on farms within driving distance of the market. That means less energy was needed to bring the foods there. They won't have as many chemicals because they don't need to stay fresh for a long journey.

Farmers' markets often
sell fruits, vegetables,
and other items outdoors.

THINK ORGANICALLY!

Buy organic foods whenever you can. Organic food comes from crops or livestock raised without chemicals. Organic food is usually labeled at grocery stores. In the fruits and vegetables area, there should be a section of organically grown food. Ask your parents to pick items from there.

WHY?

Farmers who grow organic crops do not use chemical fertilizers, weed killers, or pest control. They fertilize their fields with natural products, like seed meal and minerals. They use natural **compost**. They do not give their livestock antibiotics or other drugs. This is better for the soil and water. It is also healthier for people.

SCHOOLYARDS YOU CAN EAT

Kids at city schools are getting more opportunities to learn about farming. About half of the public schools in Chicago, Illinois, have gardens where students can grow organic vegetables. The Edible Schoolyard program at the Martin Luther King Jr. Middle School in Berkeley, California, lets kids plant, care for, and pick crops. The students can then prepare meals in a school kitchen with the food they grow.

MAKE A MEAL FROM LOCAL INGREDIENTS

Find a fun recipe and ask a grown-up if he or she will help you make it. Then, see if you can buy all the ingredients grown locally. You can visit a farmers' market for vegetables and fruits. Some grocery stores also have locally grown food sections. Before you know it, you'll have a local, homemade meal!

WHY?

The planes, trains, and trucks that transport food use gasoline. The burned gasoline releases carbon dioxide into the air. Carbon dioxide is a **greenhouse gas** that contributes to **global warming**.

Pick a recipe and see if you can buy all ingredients locally to make your healthful meal.

PLANT YOUR OWN FOOD

Plant some tomatoes in your backyard or on your porch. Tomatoes grow well in full sun in a big flowerpot. You can buy a young tomato plant from a garden center. Move it to your flowerpot. Be sure to water your plant each day. When the plant grows taller, tie it to a stick to keep it standing up straight. Record how long it takes for your first tomato to appear.

WHY?

When you eat food that you've grown, you have been in charge of how it grows. You can decide to grow it naturally instead of using chemical fertilizer. This is better for your body and for Earth.

Planting your own food is a fun way to make sure it is grown naturally.

STUDENT FARMERS

Bringing fresh foods to needy families is a goal of the Rhode Island Community Food Bank. The food is grown in community gardens. The gardens give students from local schools a chance to learn how food grows and to help the food bank. Students from the Cumberland Middle School planted more than 1,500 vegetables in one day. Those vegetables included tomatoes, peppers, onions, eggplant, cucumbers, and squash.

TIP #5

MAKE COMPOST

Do you have a garden or potted plants?
Fertilize it with compost to help things grow
better. Here's how to make your own compost:
Find a spot in your yard that is 3 square
feet (.9 m^2). Add in eggshells, apple cores,
banana peels, and other natural waste. Then
add in dead leaves, grass clippings, and soil.
Sprinkle your compost with water every few
days. Turn it every few days with a shovel or
pitchfork. In about four months, you will have
rich, crumbly soil.

WHY?

Table scraps and yard waste make up about
30 percent of the household garbage in the
United States. Most of it goes into landfills.
This food breaks down without oxygen and
creates methane. This is a greenhouse gas that
contributes to global warming.

Orange peels, eggshells, twigs, leaves, and grass can be added to compost.

EAT IN SEASON

Try to eat only the fruits and vegetables that are in season and from your area. In the Midwest, late summer is the time to pick and eat corn. In the Pacific Northwest, fall is the season for apples. Strawberries appear in many parts of the country only in late spring. You can still have these fruits and vegetables at other times of year by freezing or canning them.

WHY?

A truck that carries strawberries grown in California to a grocery store in Massachusetts sends a lot of carbon dioxide into the air. Eating fruits and vegetables that are in season from your area means less driving and less carbon dioxide exhaust. This helps prevent global warming.

Can the vegetables and fruits you aren't going to eat right away.

MAKE A MOTHER'S OR FATHER'S DAY HERB GARDEN

Instead of buying a card or gift, plant an herb garden for your mom or dad. Rosemary, dill, basil, and parsley are great plants for a small herb garden. You can grow herbs from seeds or buy starter plants from your local garden center. Find a sunny place for your Mother's or Father's Day herb garden to grow. Fertilize your herbs with soil from your compost pile.

WHY?

A total of about 2.6 billion holiday cards are sold each year in the United States. Some moms and dads keep their cards. But many millions of these cards end up in the trash.

Fresh herbs add great flavor to foods and can be grown in flowerpots or in a sunny garden.

19

PICK YOUR OWN

If you want to be sure your fruits and vegetables are fresh, look for a farm or an orchard that lets you pick your own. Many orchards will let you pick strawberries, blueberries, or apples when these fruits are in season. You can eat them fresh or turn them into a yummy pie.

WHY?

Instead of buying foods from far away, buy locally grown foods when they are in season. This saves energy and supports local farmers. Can or freeze fresh foods to eat in the off-season.

Picking apples can be a fun activity.

MAKE A LOCAL FOODS CALENDAR

Research the fruits and vegetables that grow in your area. Then make a calendar that shows when these foods are in season. Many areas have festivals centering on a local food. There are celebrations for all kinds of foods, from asparagus to zucchini. The festivals have parades, entertainment, and unusual recipes. Is there a local food festival near you?

WHY?

Buying fruits and vegetables from local farms helps the local economy. When a farmer sells a crop to food processors, the farmer gets only about 20 cents per dollar spent on food. The other 80 cents is spent on shipping, processing, packaging, and marketing. Buying foods from local farmers gives back the full value of the food to the farmer.

Write on the calendar to remind yourself when certain foods are in season.

URBAN ROOTS

Teenagers in Austin, Texas, can work for a growing season at Urban Roots, an organic farming program. In February, they begin planting after school and on Saturdays. During the summer, they work seven hours each day. The students see the vegetables in every stage of growth—from seed to fully grown plant.

TIP #10

VISIT A LOCAL FARM

Ask your teacher to organize a field trip to a local farm. This is a great way to see first-hand where your food comes from. Choose a farm that has fruits or vegetables to sample. Or, try to find a farm that also raises chickens, cows, or other animals. Then you can see where eggs, milk, and other animal products come from.

WHY?

The more you learn about farming and local foods, the better you will be at making good choices about the food you eat. There is no better way to learn than visiting a real farm. If your class cannot go to a farm, invite a farmer to come to your class and share what it is like to be a farmer.

Taking a field trip to a local farm lets you see up close where your milk, eggs, and vegetables come from.

NO FAST FOOD

What do you get when you order a fast-food meal? With your burger, french fries, and soft drink, you get a lot of packaging. Your meal comes with cardboard boxes, paper wrappers and bags, wax-coated cups, and plastic lids and straws. All of these items end up in landfills. Choose instead to make your own sandwiches and carry them in reusable containers.

WHY?

Items used only once are big contributors to the trash problem in the United States. Each year, Americans throw away enough paper and plastic cups, forks, and spoons to go around Earth at the equator 300 times. Items used only once make up about one-third of the garbage in landfills. Between 30 and 40 percent of all the trash comes from food and other kinds of packaging.

Fast-food packaging creates a lot of waste that heads to the landfills.

TIP #12

MEATLESS MONDAYS!

Did you know it takes more energy and resources to raise animals than to grow plants for food? Some people choose not to eat meat because they don't want to eat animals. Others don't eat meat for health reasons. But you can join in, too, even if you like meat. Plan one night a week to not eat meat. Help your parents find meatless recipes to make. Pastas and bean dishes are good places to start.

WHY?

Animals used for meat must eat large amounts of grain. They eat more of it than people eat. Animals eat up to 16 pounds (7.3 kg) of grain to make one pound of meat. More than 70 percent of grains grown on US farms get fed to animals that provide meat. Most of that grain is grown on large corporate farms.

By cutting out meat one day a week, you'll reduce the amount of grain, water, and land used to raise animals for food.

MORE WAYS TO GO GREEN

1. **Organize** students in your school to plant a garden on a section of the school grounds.

2. **Have** a grown-up take you on an outing to pick your own strawberries or blueberries.

3. **Ask** your parents to only buy free-range chicken and eggs and grass-fed beef and pork. These animals are allowed to roam free rather than live in coops and pens.

4. **Have** a piece of fresh, locally grown fruit for dessert instead of prepackaged, processed cookies, pie, or cake.

5. **When** your family eats out at a restaurant, pick one that is known for cooking locally grown food.

6. **Ask** your family to buy food from farm stands around town that sell fresh food.

7. **Learn** about sources of protein that are not meat, such as beans and nuts.

8. **Turn** off the television while you are eating and think about your food and where it came from.

9. **If** your community does not have a farmers' market, check your local supermarket for locally grown food. If there is none, ask the store manager to buy some items from local farms.

10. **Cook** your own meals. You can help an adult cook or find recipes. Cooking can be easy and fun. And, it lets you use locally grown food and less packaging.

compost (KOM-pohst): Compost is a mixture of leaves, old food scraps, and soil that is used to fertilize plants and land. Using compost prevents chemicals from going into the ground.

factory farms (FAK-tuh-ree FARMS): Factory farms are farms where many animals are raised, usually in tight quarters. Factory farms often give animals antibiotics.

farmers' market (FARM-urs MAR-kit): A farmers' market is where farmers sell their products directly to shoppers. A farmers' market is a great place to buy locally grown food.

global warming (GLOHB-ul WOR-ming): Global warming is the heating up of Earth's atmosphere and oceans due to air pollution. Too much carbon dioxide in the air contributes to global warming.

greenhouse gas (GREEN-houss GASS): A greenhouse gas is a gas like carbon dioxide or methane that helps hold heat in the atmosphere. Too much greenhouse gas in the atmosphere causes global warming.

organic (or-GAN-ik): If something is organic, it is grown, raised, or made without the use of artificial chemicals. A good way to eat right for you and the Earth is to eat organic foods.

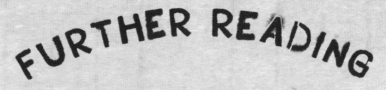

FURTHER READING

BOOKS

Cooper, Elisha. *Farm*. London: Orchard Books, 2010.

Nagra, Anne. *Our Super Garden: Learning the Power of Healthy Eating*. Wilmette, IL: Dancing Rhinoceros Press, 2010.

Peterson, Cris. *Seed, Soil, Sun*. Honesdale, PA: Boyds Mills Press, 2010.

WEB SITES

Visit our Web site for links about good food that is good for Earth:
http://www.childsworld.com/links

Note to Parents, Teachers, and Librarians: We routinely verify our Web links to make sure they are safe and active sites. So encourage your readers to check them out!

INDEX